For Woody, Amy, Ben & Rory

Copyright © 2016 by Andrea Zuill

Visit us on the Web! randomhousekids.com

Educators and librarians, for a variety of teaching tools, visit us at RHTeachersLibrarians.com

Library of Congress Cataloging-in-Publication Data
Zuill, Andrea, author, illustrator.
Wolf camp / Andrea Zuill. —First edition.
pages cm
Summary: "Homer the dog goes away to wolf camp to learn how to bring out his inner wolf" —Provided by publisher.
ISBN 978-0-553-50912-0 (hardback) — ISBN 978-0-553-50913-7 (glb) — ISBN 978-0-553-50914-4 (ebook)
[1. Dogs—Fiction. 2. Wolves—Fiction. 3. Camps—Fiction.] I. Title.
PZ7.1.Z83Wo 2016
[E]—dc23
2015018906

The text of this book is set in P22 Sherwood.
The illustrations were rendered in pen-and-ink and watercolor and digitally manipulated using Adobe Photoshop.
Book design by Rachael Cole

MANUFACTURED IN CHINA
2 4 6 8 10 9 7 5 3 1
First Edition

WOLF CAMP

Andrea Zuill

schwartz & wade books · new york

My name is Homer. I am a dog . . .

... but sometimes I am very wolfish.

All dogs have a bit of wolf in them. It's been proven by science.

(This scene may not have actually happened.)

Often I've wondered what it would be
like to live as a real wolf.

Then one day I got a surprise.

WOLF CAMP

HAVE YOU EVER FELT LIKE HOWLING AT THE MOON?

COME JOIN US!

WOLF CAMP

Where every dog can live as a wolf—for an entire week!

for information call:

1-800-WOLF-CAMP

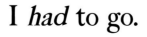

I *had* to go.

And after a while,

my people thought I should go, too.

The day finally arrived, and I was off!

Then I got to know my fellow campers.

Fang gave us an important safety talk.

At last we were ready to be real wolves.

We marked,

howled,

and tracked.

The big moment was here. It was time to hunt!

Dinner tasted unusual.

Before bed I wrote
a letter home.

Dear People,
How are you?
I am fine. The food
here is yucky and has
hair on it. So please
send me some of
Grandma Polly's Pampered
Pooch Doggie Snacks, the
bacon-flavored ones.
Also, send my flea medicine
because there are a lot
of bugs and they are
gross.
Love,
Homer

Smashed Bug

When it got dark, we found out how real wolves sleep.

I was starting to miss home.

Fortunately, with each day we adjusted to life in the wild.

By the end of camp we were practically wolves.

We were given the certificates to prove it.

Now that it was time to leave, I was feeling a little sad. (I don't think anyone noticed.)

We howled one last time as a pack.

It was good to be home.

Homer!

But I had changed. I was no longer plain old Homer. . . .